SO-CKI-280

41188 ·   j811

Monjo

The sea beggar's son

NO LONGER THE PROPERTY OF KIRKWOOD PUBLIC LIBRARY

KIRKWOOD PUBLIC LIBRARY

PROPERTY OF

The
Sea Beggar's
Son

NORTH SEA

ZUIDER ZEE

W E S

Alkmaar

Haarlem

Leyden

Amsterdam

The Hague

Delft

Dort

Utrecht

Brill

Bergen op Zoom

Breda

To Flushing and Sluys

Antwerp

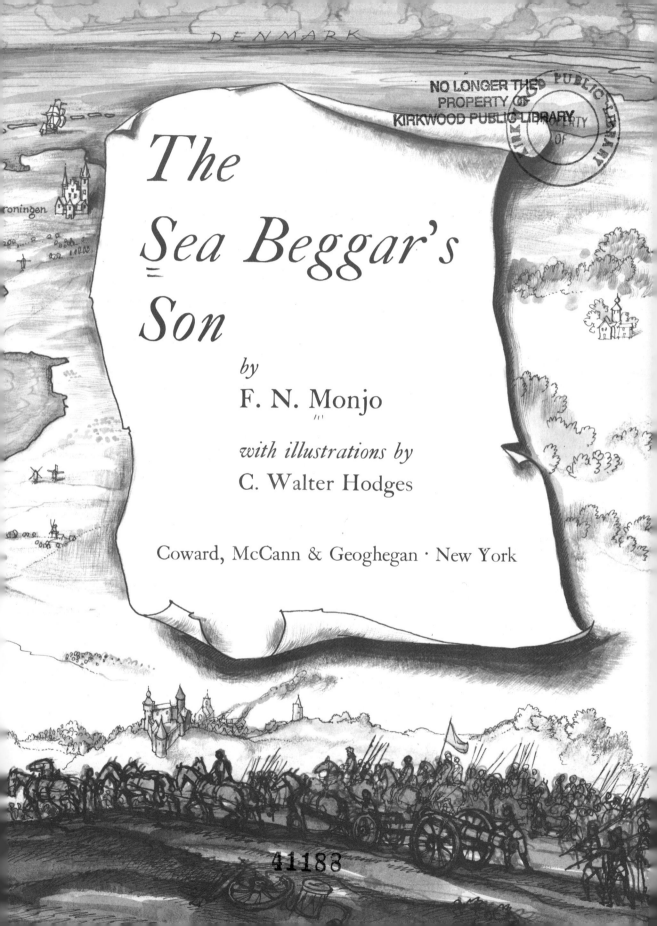

The Sea Beggar's Son

by

F. N. Monjo

with illustrations by

C. Walter Hodges

Coward, McCann & Geoghegan · New York

NO LONGER THE PROPERTY OF KIRKWOOD PUBLIC LIBRARY

KIRKWOOD PUBLIC LIBRARY

41183

Text copyright © 1974 by F. N. Monjo
Illustrations copyright © 1974 by C. Walter Hodges
All rights reserved.
This book, or parts thereof, may not be reproduced
in any form without permission in writing from the publishers.
Published simultaneously in Canada by
Longman Canada Limited, Toronto.
SBN: GB-698-30529-9
SBN: TR-698-20277-5
Library of Congress Catalog Card Number: 73-78320
PRINTED IN GREAT BRITAIN
07212

Piet Heyn was a Dutchman,
A Dutchman from Delft,
Who braved the blue deeps of the sea,
To sail out, seafaring,
For flounder and herring,
While he dreamed that his land might be free.

For the Dutch were then ruled
By King Philip of Spain,
And a dark, cruel master was he,
Who forbade them to pray
In their own simple way
And who taxed them all mercilessly.

Dutch women were buried
In graves, alive,
If they angered their royal sire.
And should Dutchmen not pray
In King Philip's way,
He burned them alive in the fire.

The drums beat—*van dirra,*
Van dirra, van dyne.
The Spanish troops marched, to each village and town.
But the Dutch meant to fight,
So they slammed their gates tight
And fought on their walls, till their walls were smashed down.

"I remember," said Piet,

As he mended his nets,

With his young son, Piet, by his side,

"How our William of Orange,

Dutch Prince William of Orange,

Lent all of us beggars some pluck and some pride!

"Ja! They called us all 'Beggars,'

The Spaniards did!

They said, 'Spain has nothing to fear.

Poor Dutchmen, so humble,

May riot and grumble,

But they'll never fight free of Spain here!'

"Prince William of Orange
Knew what we must do—
On land, he could see, we were beaten and torn.
So 'twas William's decree
That we take to the sea.
And so the Sea Beggars were born.

"Sea Beggars, young Piet!
You've heard that name?
We battered Spain's ships and took their supplies.
And their ships that weren't sinking
Crept, leaking and slinking,
To Antwerp and Flushing and Sluys.

"Once more Philip's soldiers
Surrounded our towns.
The drums beat—*van dirra-don-dee.*
Haarlem was lost
At terrible cost.
But Leyden was saved—by the sea!

"William's carrier pigeons
Flew all of his messages
Over the walls, in those desperate days.
His birds fluttered down
Into Leyden town,
Bringing plans and more plans, and comfort and praise.

"After six months of siege
They were hungry in Leyden,
And they feared they must soon haul their brave banners down.
But William said, 'No!
The sea dikes must go!
The Spaniards will have to retreat, or they'll drown.'

"So we cut the great dikes,
And the sea waves rolled in.
We Sea Beggars rode them right in, on the tide,
Bringing meat and bread
(As the Spanish troops fled)
For all of the folks who were starving inside.

"And the bells rang loud
To tell the brave news:
Van dingle, van dongle, van dyne!
'Sea Beggars, hooray!'
The bells seemed to say
To your Sea Beggar father, Piet Heyn, my boy,
To this old herring fisherman, Heyn!"

Now, of course, young Piet
Couldn't wait to grow up
And set sail, for himself, on the brine.
"Ja, a bold life at sea
Is the best life for me!"
Said salty Piet Pieterzoon Heyn.

So Dutch Piet from Delft,
The Sea Beggar's son,
Grew up, and he sailed off to sea.
With might and main
He fought against Spain
And he fought to make Holland free.

He joined the Dutch Navy
And scoured the New World,
Seeking King Philip's ships from the rich Spanish Main.
And Piet managed to get
Fifty-five in his net!
And to sail them back, captive, to Holland again.

But they caught him at last,
The Spaniards did,
And Piet slaved in their galleys, chained fast to an oar.
For three years, and four,
He sweated and swore
That once he was ransomed, he'd fight them some more.

So, when Piet was set free,

The Dutch gave him a fleet,

And he said, "We'll be clever and daring.

Then, if we're plucky,

And patient, and lucky,

We'll catch something *better* than herring."

So said the Sea Beggar's son, Dutch Piet,

So said Piet Pieterzoon Heyn.

Now Spain owned rich mines of silver and gold
In Mexico and Peru,
And when Philip's great fleet would appear,
It could hardly hold
All the silver and gold
Dug from those mines every year.

The king's ships groaned
With gold, silver, and pearls,
With barrels of spices and bright crimson dye,
And their sails would strain
For faraway Spain,
Their holds and their decks piled high.

All this treasure
King Philip would spend
In fighting his terrible fights:
Killing the Dutch,
With burning, and such,
And taking away their rights.

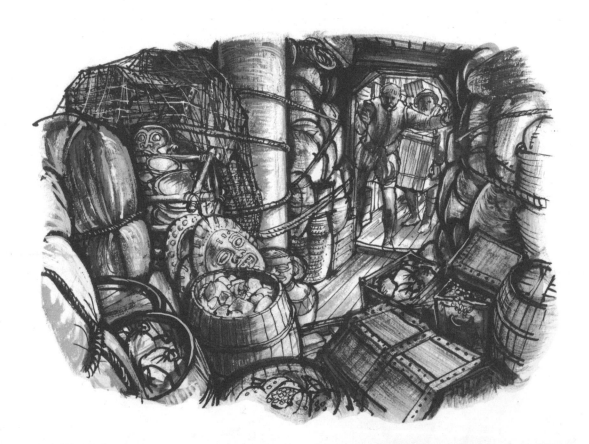

But Piet Pieterzoon Heyn
Had gone to sea
With Dutch ships and Dutch courage abounding.
And he wanted to meet
The king's treasure fleet—
To give it a terrible pounding!

Well, meet it he did,
Not far from Havana,
In the Bay of Matanzas, the eighth of September.
And Piet had his way
That glorious day,
In a fight that all Dutchmen will always remember.

The Spanish ships raced
For the fort, in the bay,
Racing for safety, under the guns.
But soon they found
They'd run aground,
Weighed down by the treasure they measured in tons.

For when Piet hove in sight,

And the Spanish turned tail,

Their keels grated fast in the sands.

And the silver and gold

In each heavy ship's hold

Fell into the Dutchman's hands,

Fell into the hands of the Dutchman from Delft,

The Sea Beggar's son, Piet Heyn.

The whole Spanish fleet

Was caught by Dutch Piet!

And the Spaniard must pay the cost.

For though Philip must rage

Like a bear in a cage,

Every penny he needed was lost!

And Piet Pieterzoon Heyn
Stowed his treasure on board
And sailed away over the foam
With King Philip's millions,
Fifteen Spanish millions,
Chinking, below, as he headed for home!

Piet sailed back, quite safe,
And all Holland went wild.
Bells rang: *van dingle, van doom!*
In Groningen, *gong!*
In Amsterdam, *clong!*
In Dort, they rang *cling!*
In Delft, they rang *clang!*
And in Bergen op Zoom they rang *bong!*

Drums kept beating at Breda;
They beat at The Hague;
Bells were ringing in Alkmaar, and Utrecht, and Brill.
Bonfires bright
Burned bold through the night,
And the trumpets and fifes sounded shrill.

41188

NO LONGER THE PROPERTY KIRKWOOD PUBLIC LIBRARY

All sounding for Piet,

Who had captured the fleet

With its silver and gold from King Philip's dark mines!

For Piet, who saved Holland!

Long live old Holland!

And long live Piet Pieterzoon Heyn!

Long live Dutch Piet, the Sea Beggar's son,

The Dutchman from Delft,

Piet Heyn!

PIET PIETERZOON HEYN

NO LONGER THE
PROPERTY OF
KIRKWOOD PUBLIC LIBRARY

ABOUT THESE VERSES

PIET HEYN the Younger (Pieter Pieterzoon Heyn, 1578-1629), was the son of Pieter Heyn, a herring fisherman of Delft. It is not certain that the elder Piet ever was a Sea Beggar, though it seems likely. His son, an admiral in the Dutch Navy, became one of Holland's most famous heroes.

He went to sea as a young man, was captured by the Spaniards, and was sentenced to four years in the galleys. After his release he went back to sea, and from 1621 to 1628 he and his sailors captured no fewer than fifty-five Spanish ships off the coast of Brazil and in the Caribbean. On September 8, 1628, he captured all fifteen vessels of the Spanish "silver fleet" near Havana.

Piet's victory gave Holland the courage—and the money—to fight on, and the country went wild with rejoicing; a day of thanksgiving was celebrated with the ringing of church bells, bonfires, and the crowning of Piet with a gilded laurel crown. When he died, a year later, in a daring attack on pirate ships off Dunkirk, he was universally mourned. He was buried in Delft.

The formation of the Sea Beggars (1564) and the siege of Leyden (1574) took place some years before Piet Heyn the Younger was born, in the days of Holland's great patriot, William the Silent, Prince of Orange (1533-1584), whose quarrel with King Philip II of Spain began in 1568.

Philip II was indeed a cruel and unforgiving monarch—particularly where his Dutch subjects were concerned. He hated Protestants, and when images and windows in Roman Catholic cathedrals and churches in Antwerp and Holland were smashed by Calvinists in 1566, Philip vowed revenge. In 1567 he sent the Duke of Alba with an army to the Netherlands, with full power to execute Protestants (Anabaptists, Calvinists, Lutherans), and the duke hanged and beheaded and burned and buried thousands alive, as well as besieging and decimating any walled towns that resisted his authority.

The following year he sent the Duke of Alba with an army to the Netherlands, and the duke waged a violent and bloody campaign against all who resisted his authority.

It was William of Orange who roused his countrymen and began the revolt against Spain. He was assisted by privateers, contemptuously named by the Spaniards Sea Beggars. William was assassinated in 1584 by one of Philip's agents, and it was not until 1648, after eighty years of struggle, that Holland achieved its independence.

If the Dutch had not succeeded in gaining religious toleration for themselves, that principle might not have taken hold as soon as it did in England or America. And if the Dutch had not shown how a small federation of states might unite to gain its freedom from a great power, the young United States might never have dared to push its quarrel with England to a successful conclusion.

I borrowed the meter and the sound of the beating of the drum from a Dutch ballad (written in the sixteenth century) quoted by John Lothrop Motley in his classic history *The Rise of the Dutch Republic.* The first two lines are as follows:

> *Slaet op den tromele, van dirre dom deyne,*
> *Slaet op den tromele, van dirre dom does . . .*